Hana
the Hanukkah
Fairy

By Daisy Meadows

ORCHARD

www.rainbowmagicbooks.co.uk

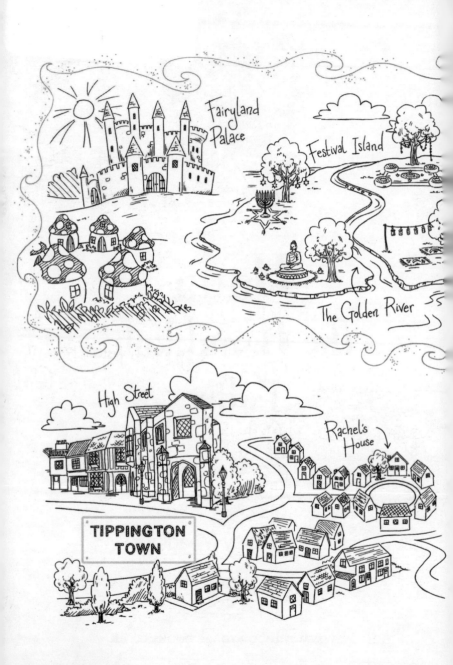

We hope you enjoy this book.
Please return or renew it by the due date.
You can renew it at **www.norfolk.gov.uk/libraries**
or by using our free library app. Otherwise you can
phone **0344 800 8020** - please have your library
card and pin ready.
You can sign up for email reminders too.

NORFOLK COUNTY COUNCIL
LIBRARY AND INFORMATION SERVICE

This book is worth 1 star.

To Selma, with love

Special thanks to Rachel Elliot
With thanks to Anna Solemani
for her input

ORCHARD BOOKS

First published in Great Britain in 2020 by The Watts Publishing Group

1 3 5 7 9 10 8 6 4 2

© 2020 Rainbow Magic Limited
© 2020 HIT Entertainment Limited
Illustrations © 2020 The Watts Publishing Group Limited

HIT entertainment

A CIP catalogue record for this book is available from the British Library.

ISBN 978 1 40836 238 9

Printed and bound in Great Britain by Clays Ltd, Elcograf S.p.A.

MIX
Paper from
responsible sources
FSC
www.fsc.org
FSC® C104740

The paper and board used in this book are made from wood from responsible sources

Orchard Books
An imprint of Hachette Children's Group
Part of The Watts Publishing Group Limited
Carmelite House, 50 Victoria Embankment, London EC4Y 0DZ

An Hachette UK Company
www.hachette.co.uk
www.hachettechildrens.co.uk

Jack Frost's Ice Castle

Jack Frost's Festival Tent

WETHERBURY

Kirsty's House

Jack Frost's Spell

Ignore Eid and Buddha Day.
Make Diwali go away.
Scrap Hanukkah and make them see –
They should be celebrating me!

I'll steal ideas and spoil their fun.
My Frost Day plans have just begun.
Bring gifts and sweets to celebrate
The many reasons I'm so great!

Contents

Chapter One
Sneaky Goblins

"Five snow fairies," said Rachel Walker in a delighted voice. "This is the most snow we've ever had in Tippington."

Her best friend, Kirsty Tate, rubbed the snow off her mittens and smiled. She had come to stay with Rachel after the end of the autumn term. They had spent all

afternoon building the snow fairies, and it was starting to get dark.

"I wish they were real," Kirsty said.

Being together again had given them a chance to talk about their most recent adventure in Fairyland. Jack Frost had stolen the magical objects that belonged to the Festival Fairies. He was planning

his own festival, which he called Frost
Day, and he wanted to steal as many
ideas he could from Diwali, Hanukkah,
Eid and Buddha Day.

Rachel and Kirsty had helped Deena
the Diwali Fairy to get her diya back,
but there were still three magical objects
missing, and three other fairies whose
festivals were in danger.

"I really thought we'd have a visit from
Hana the Hanukkah Fairy," said Rachel.

Hanukkah, the Jewish Festival of Light,
was nearly over, and they hadn't seen
a single speck of magic. The girls didn't
know when – or if – Hana would need
them.

The back door opened, and Mr Walker
came out carrying a box.

"Girls, would you take this over to

Abigail's house?" he said. "I promised her dad I'd make some doughnuts for their Hannukah celebrations tonight. They said you could stay for the ceremony if you like."

"Yes please," said Rachel.

"What kind of doughnuts?" said Kirsty, peeping into the box. "Oh, jam. Yum!"

"In Hebrew, they are called 'sufganiyot'," said Mr Walker. "I believe that there are all sorts of delicious things to eat at a Hanukkah party."

Eagerly, the girls took the box and walked down the street. Snow started to fall again.

"Is Abigail in your class?" Kirsty asked.

"No, she goes to a different school," said Rachel. "But our dads are friends, so we play together sometimes."

Abigail lived in a tall, red-brick house on the corner of the street. Rachel and Kirsty ran up the steps and knocked on the green wooden door. They heard running footsteps, and then the door was flung open by a slim girl with bobbed black hair.

"Hello Rachel! Are those the

sufganiyot?" she asked. "My favourite!"

"This is my best friend, Kirsty," said
Rachel. "She's staying with me for a few
days."

Just then there was a burst of singing
from inside the house. Abigail smiled.

"Come in," she said. "We're setting
out the food for the party later. Lots of
people are coming over to celebrate the
eighth night of Hanukkah."

"Thanks, we'd love to," said Rachel.

They kicked the snow off their boots,
pulled off their woolly hats and stepped
inside. Abigail took them to the kitchen,
where they met her mum and dad, and
her little sister Miriam. The house was
decorated with hundreds of tiny lights.

"It reminds me of Diwali," said Kirsty,
remembering the little lanterns that her

friend Kirin had strung around his house.

"Yes, they're both festivals of lights," said Abigail's mum. "Hanukkah celebrates a victory and a miracle in Jewish history."

Miriam tugged at their sleeves.

"Would you like to play dreidel with me?" she asked.

"I'd like to, but I don't know how," said Kirsty. "Will you show us?"

The girls put the sufganiyot on a large plate. Then Miriam pulled them into the sitting room. The first thing they saw was a special candle holder on a table by the window.

"That reminds me of Hana the Hanukkah fairy's magical object," Kirsty whispered in Rachel's ear. "It looks just the same."

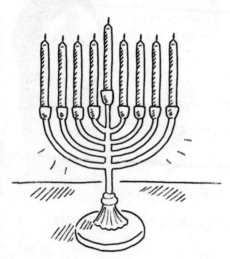

"That's our hanukkiah," Abigail explained. "It holds nine candles in a row, and we light an extra candle for every night of Hanukkah."

"I thought Hanukkah lasted for eight nights," said Rachel. "Why are there nine candles?"

"The space in the middle is for the helper candle," said Abigail. "We use it to light the others."

Miriam showed them a small spinning top with four sides.

"This is the dreidel," she said, giving it a spin.

"There are lots of traditions around Hanukkah," said Abigail. "We always play dreidel with the grown-ups."

"And there are presents," said Miriam, spinning the dreidel again. "Don't forget those!"

"Yes, our family give gifts every night of Hanukkah," said Abigail, smiling at her excited little sister.

"Chocolate coins and books and games," said Miriam, twirling around. "And the yummiest food. My favourites are the doughnuts."

Abigail handed Rachel a dreidel.

"Here, you have a turn," she said.

"Miriam, Abigail," called their mum from the kitchen. "Could you come and take a few plates through, please?"

The sisters hurried out and Rachel and Kirsty practised spinning the dreidel. Then the sitting room door creaked and someone giggled. The girls looked up,

expecting
to see
Abigail and
Miriam.
Instead,
they saw a
mischievous
green face
peeping
around the
door at
them.

"Oh my
goodness,"
said Kirsty.
"That's a
goblin!"

Chapter Two
New Orders

A second green face peered around the
door. He stuck out his tongue at the
girls. Rachel leapt towards the door and
the faces disappeared. By the time she
reached the hallway, the goblins had
vanished.

"We have to find them," said Rachel.

"What do you think they are doing here?"

"Something naughty," said Kirsty, joining her in the hallway.

They could hear Abigail and her family laughing in the kitchen.

"Abigail would have seen them if they had gone in there," said Rachel. "Perhaps they're upstairs."

The girls stood at the bottom of the stairs and looked up. There were no lights on.

"It would be rude to go upstairs without asking permission," said Kirsty. "But they are bound to ask us why we want to go up there."

"We can't lie," said Rachel. "But we can't tell them the truth either. Oh dear."

They had promised Queen Titania

never to tell anyone about Fairyland
or magic, and that included the goblins
and Jack Frost. They couldn't break their
promise.

Just then, there was a scuffling noise
from the landing upstairs.

"That's them," said Kirsty. "I'm sure of
it."

"Goblins," said Rachel in her loudest
whisper. "Please come down. You
shouldn't be up there."

There was another scuffling sound, and
then a tall goblin appeared at the top of
the stairs with a yellow rucksack in his
hand. He sat down and crossed his legs.

"What do you want?" he asked.

"It's not polite to wander around in
somebody's house without being invited,"
said Rachel.

The goblin blew a loud raspberry at her.

"What are you doing here?" asked Kirsty.

"Wouldn't you like to know?" the goblin retorted.

"You're being rude," said Rachel.

The goblin threw back his head and burst out laughing.

"Don't you get it?" he said. "We're here to be rude."

"What do you mean?" asked Kirsty.

"We're on a mission to cause as much trouble as we can," said the goblin with an unpleasant grin. "It's fun."

The girls exchanged worried looks.

"Jack Frost has Hana's magical hanukkiah," said Rachel. "We guessed that he would do something to spoil Hanukkah."

"He doesn't care about spoiling Hanukkah," sneered the goblin.

Rachel and Kirsty shared another worried look. If Jack Frost didn't want to spoil Hanukkah, why had he sent the goblins here?"

"But you must have been sent to take Hanukkah ideas," Kirsty stammered.

"If we see something that should belong to Frost Day, we'll take it," said the goblin. "But Jack Frost wants to get his own back on you."

"On us?" asked Rachel.

"He hasn't forgotten that you helped that silly Diwali fairy to get her lamp back," said the goblin with a sneer.

Just then, the sitting room door creaked. The goblin let out a squawk of laughter.

"What's so funny?" asked Kirsty.

The goblin just hugged his rucksack and darted out of sight. Just then, Miriam came out of the kitchen with the doughnuts that the girls had brought. Abigail and her parents were close behind, also carrying large plates of food.

"Here we are," said Abigail's mum. "Latkes, sufganiyot, blintzes—"

She stopped as she walked into the sitting room.

"Where are the candles?" she asked.

Rachel and Kirsty ran in. The family's hanukkiah was empty.

"This was that naughty goblin's plan all along," whispered Kirsty. "He kept us talking while the other goblin went in and took the candles."

"Miriam, did you move them?" Abigail's mum asked, frowning a little.

Miriam shook her head, and her mum turned to Rachel and Kirsty with raised eyebrows.

"It wasn't us, we promise," said Rachel.

Even though she was innocent, she felt bad. She wished that she could tell the whole truth.

"We can't celebrate Hanukkah without the candles," said Abigail, her lips trembling.

"I'm sure we'll find them," said her mum. "I can't understand what's happened, but we won't let it spoil

Hanukkah."

"We'll look for
them," said Kirsty,
pulling Rachel
out of the room.

There were
no goblins in the
kitchen, so the girls
went into the larder. It

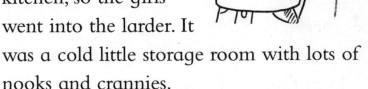

was a cold little storage room with lots of
nooks and crannies.

"They could easily have hidden the
candles in here," said Rachel, shutting the
door.

The girls searched everywhere. They
peeped behind large bags of rice and big
tubs of honey. But there was not a candle
to be seen.

"Let's check the garden," said Rachel.

Kirsty went to open the larder door, but the handle wouldn't turn.

"It's stuck," she said.

Even with both of them trying, it wouldn't budge.

"This door isn't just stuck," said Rachel. "We've been locked in."

Chapter Three
Inside the Dreidel

A stifled giggle came from the other side of the door.

"This is the best plan we've ever had," someone said in a squawky voice.

"Open this door," Rachel said through the keyhole.

Kirsty looked around for another way

out, but there was no window and no
other door. They were trapped.

"We can't shout for help," she said. "If
anyone comes, they'll see the goblins
outside the door."

The girls sat down on the tiled floor.
Rachel was still holding the dreidel.

"What are we going to do?" she asked,
spinning the dreidel on the tiles.

"There's only one thing we can do,"
said Kirsty.

She reached for the locket that always
hung around her neck. Queen Titania
had given one to each of the girls. There
was just enough fairy dust inside for one
trip to Fairyland. The dreidel clattered
down and lay still. Kirsty picked it up
and spun it.

"The queen told us to use them

whenever we need help," she said. "If we don't stop those goblins, they might be seen and that will definitely spoil Hanukkah for your friend."

Rachel was staring at the dreidel.

"That must have been a really good spin," she said. "It's still going."

"I think it's getting faster," said Kirsty. "And it's sparkling."

In the dim larder light, the dreidel was dazzling.

"I don't think we're going to need to use the fairy dust," said Rachel in an excited voice. "That's magic."

The four sides of the dreidel suddenly sprang open, and Hana the Hanukkah Fairy stood there beaming at them. Rachel felt her heart thump with excitement.

"Hi, Hana!" she said. "It's great to see you!"

Hana was wearing a powder-blue dress with filmy sleeves and a petal-shaped hem. Her dark, wavy hair was tucked loosely behind her ears, and dimples appeared in her cheeks as she smiled at them. Quickly, they told her everything that had happened. Hana flew to the door and peeped through the keyhole.

"The goblins aren't there," she said. "I can use my magic to unlock the door."

"Hana, can you turn us into fairies?" said Rachel. "We'll search more quickly if we can fly."

Hana raised her wand and gave it a little shake. Golden flakes of fairy dust floated around the girls, settling on their hair and eyelashes. A magical glow lit up the little larder.

"I'm tingling all over," said Rachel.

"I love turning into a fairy," said Kirsty. "However many times it happens, it's always so exciting."

In the blink of an eye, they had shrunk to the same size as Hana. Their filmy wings unfurled and fluttered.

"I'm glad to have your help," said

Hana, giving them a hug. "Now, let's get out of this cupboard."

It was easy to slip out through the gap

at the top of the door. The kitchen was empty, but loud voices were coming from the sitting room.

The fairies flew to the door and looked through the crack. Inside, Abigail and

Miriam were arguing with someone.

"That's not fair," they heard Abigail say.

"Why are you being so mean?" asked
Miriam.

"Who are they talking to?" asked
Kirsty. "I can't see."

Rachel flew up to perch on the top of
the door. Then she gasped.

"Oh my goodness," she said. "You're not going to believe this, but they're talking to people who look exactly like us!"

Chapter Four
Copy Me, Copy You

Hana and Kirsty flew up to join Rachel. Someone who looked very like Kirsty was lying on the sofa, and a version of Rachel was by the window, trying to balance on one leg. They were wearing the same clothes as Rachel and Kirsty, and the girls' woolly hats were pulled low over their faces. Abigail was looking at them both with her hands on her hips.

"I don't understand," she said. "I thought you were going to help us look for the candles."

"Candles are boring," said the fake Rachel. "Use a lamp."

"The hanukkiah is an important part of our traditions," said Abigail. "And I thought we were friends."

"Abigail is going to think I'm really mean," exclaimed the real Rachel.

"Who are they?" asked Hana.

"They must be the goblins," said Kirsty. "Look at that yellow rucksack next to the sofa. It's the same one that the tall goblin was carrying earlier on. Besides, I think they're wearing wigs."

"Goblins don't like human beings," said Hana. "Why would they want to look like you?"

"Only Jack Frost would want them to do something as mean as this," said Kirsty. "He must have given them the orders before they left Fairyland."

"Why would he do that?" asked Hana.

"The goblin told us why," said Kirsty. "Jack Frost is cross with us because we helped Deena get her magical diya back. He wants to get his own back."

"It's working," said Rachel, her eyes filling with tears. "Abigail thinks I'm being horrible to her. I would never treat a friend like that."

"What can we do?" asked Hana. "We can't let Abigail see you like this, and you can't tell her about Fairyland."

"Don't give up," Kirsty said. "We can sort everything out if we can just get your magical object back."

Just then, the doorbell rang.

"That must be our guests," said Abigail.

As she and Miriam left the room, Miriam's foot knocked against the yellow rucksack with a *CLUNK*.

"I wonder what's in there," Rachel whispered to Hana.

Hana's eyes sparkled with hope. Could it be her hanukkiah? The fairies swooped down to the sofa and landed beside the yellow rucksack.

"Fairies!" said the fake Rachel in alarm.

The disguised goblins stuck out their tongues and pulled rude faces.

"Please stop pretending to be us," said Kirsty.

"It's fun," said the fake Kirsty. "Besides, you can't get cross with us. We're just following orders."

Out of the corner of her eye, Rachel could see Hana reaching out towards the rucksack. She had to stop the goblins from seeing what the fairy was doing.

"Following orders is wrong if the orders are wrong," she said in a gentle voice.

The disguised goblins glanced at each other and then burst out laughing.

"We like following orders, silly," the fake Rachel said. "We get to cause trouble, make mischief and send Jack Frost things for his festival. Best of all,

Jack Frost lent us enough magic to send festival things back to the Ice Castle, with the help of that candle holder he gave us. Hey!"

The Rachel goblin snatched the rucksack away from Hana and then both goblins scampered out of the room.

"I think my hanukkiah is in that rucksack," Hana whispered. "Without it, Hanukkah will be ruined."

"Follow them," said Kirsty. "We have to get that hanukkiah back – without being seen."

The guests were taking off their coats in the hallway and didn't pay attention to the disguised goblins running into the kitchen. The fairies followed and saw them crouching on the table, grabbing handfuls of food.

"These are yummy," said the fake Rachel, with sugar all around his mouth. "Let's send them to Jack Frost."

The fake Kirsty unzipped the yellow rucksack and took out a glowing golden candle holder.

"That's it!" said Hana. "That's my hanukkiah."

She waved her wand at the kitchen door and it swung shut.

"Please give that back," said Kirsty. "It doesn't belong to you."

The goblin Kirsty blew a raspberry, then touched the plate of doughnuts with

the edge of the hanukkiah. Instantly, the sweet treats disappeared.

"They must be sending everything they can to Jack Frost," said Hana with a groan. "Every time they touch something, the magic of my hanukkiah is sending it to the Ice Castle to be part of the Frost Day festival."

"Don't take anything else," pleaded Rachel.

"Leave us alone," said the Kirsty goblin. "We're going to take as much food, lights and decorations as we want, just like Jack Frost wanted to do at Diwali. And you can't stop us."

Chapter Five
Avalanche!

The Kirsty goblin waved the hanukkiah over a plate of pancakes, which vanished.

"We have to get them away from the food before they take every scrap," said Hana.

"I have an idea," said Rachel. "Maybe we can make them think that there are more decorations outside. If we can keep them there, they won't be able to bother Abigail and her family."

Hana flicked her wand. A burst of fairy dust bounced the back door open.

"Don't let them see what we've got outside," Rachel called out.

The goblins exchanged an excited look and raced out into the snowy back garden, the Kirsty goblin still clutching the hanukkiah. Hana clapped her hands, her eyes sparkling.

"It worked," she said in delight. "Now, let's keep them there."

Outside, the moon had vanished behind a cloud. The fairies fluttered away from the house and perched on top of a stone bird bath. The goblins were nowhere to be seen.

"It's too dark to see their footprints," said Kirsty. "How are we going to find them?"

"Let's listen," said Hana in a soft voice. "Goblins find it very hard to whisper. Perhaps if we can be as quiet as mice, we might hear them."

Hovering in the frosty air, the fairies

stayed as silent as they could. Rachel held her breath. Kirsty felt as if her heart was beating loudly enough for everyone to hear. They heard the screech of a nearby owl. They heard the scrunch and snuffle of a hedgehog in the snow. And then . . .

"Stop shoving me," squawked a grumpy voice.

"I've dropped my wig," hissed another. "Ooh, my head's chilly."

"Have you found anything that Jack Frost would want for Frost Day?" said the first goblin.

"I put my foot in

a lovely pile of soggy leaves just now," said the other.

"Send them," said the first goblin. "They might be part of the Hanukkah festival."

"That gives me an idea," said Kirsty. "Hana, could you light up the garden? The goblins enjoy things that are cold and wet and uncomfortable. If they can see, they might spot lots of things they like. Then, while they're distracted, we could fly up behind them and try to get the hanukkiah back."

Hana's shoulders dropped.

"I wish I could help," she said in a small voice. "But Hanukkah is a festival of lights. Without my hanukkiah, my magic isn't strong enough to light up a big space like this garden."

Tears glimmered in her eyes, and

Rachel and Kirsty rushed to give her a hug.

"It's OK," said Kirsty. "A tiny light could be even better."

"Yes," Rachel agreed. "The people in the house might notice a big light, but they won't see something fairy-sized."

Hana smiled and hugged them back. Then she lifted her wand and spoke the words of a spell:

"Glow and gleam, friendly beam.
Help us find the goblin team.
Little light, shiny bright,
It's time for us to put things right."

The tip of her wand puffed up like a tiny balloon, glowing silvery white. It was bright enough to shine a pool of light a little way ahead of them. Hana fluttered towards the goblin voices with Rachel and Kirsty behind her. They drew closer to the goblins.

"What's that light?" one goblin hissed.

"Stop grabbing my arm," grumbled the second. "It's just a silly insect buzzing around."

"No, it's following us," said the first.

The goblins were standing beside the garden shed, and one of them had the hanukkiah in his hand. They were peering through the darkness towards Hana.

"They can see the little light, but they can't see Hana carrying it," said Rachel in Kirsty's ear.

"Maybe it's something to do with the festival," said the other goblin. "Let's catch it and send it to Jack Frost!"

Hana looked at Rachel and Kirsty and her cheeks dimpled as she smiled.

"I've got an idea," she whispered. "I'm going to distract the goblins. Try to get the hanukkiah."

Holding her wand out in front of her, Hana started to dance. She twisted and tumbled through the air, up and down, left and right, and the goblins stared with open mouths. To them, it looked as if a tiny firefly was putting on an amazing show.

Rachel and Kirsty fluttered around behind the goblins. The Kirsty goblin was still holding the golden hanukkiah, but it was dangling loosely in his hand. The

yellow rucksack was on the ground, and
Rachel peeped inside.

"The Hanukkah candles are in there,"
she said. "But we can't lift them while
we're fairies. They're bigger and heavier
than us."

"So is the hanukkiah, and it's human
sized," said Kirsty. "Even if we get the
goblin to let go of it, how can we lift it
up?"

Suddenly, an idea popped into Rachel's
head.

"We can't lift it, but perhaps we can
make it heavier," she said. "Let's try to
make him drop it."

The goblins were still watching Hana
dancing with the light, making loops
and zigzags in the air. Rachel and Kirsty
swooped low and hovered on either side

of the hanukkiah. Each of them wrapped her arms around one of the golden stems. Then they both folded their wings and clung on tight.

"Oof, this stupid thing is getting too heavy," squawked the Kirsty goblin.

"Shut up," said the Rachel goblin. "You wanted to carry it."

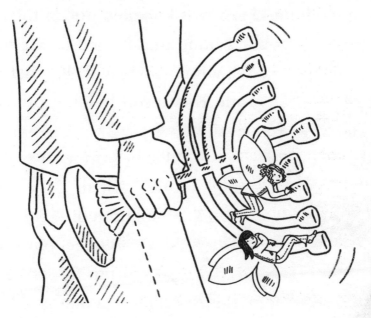

"My arms are tired," the Kirsty goblin wailed. "You take it."

"No way," said the Rachel goblin, giving him a shove.

The Kirsty goblin stumbled back and bumped into the shed. *WHUMP!* All the snow slid off the shed roof and landed right on top of the goblins. The hanukkiah was knocked out of the goblin's hand and buried under the cold, white snow, with Rachel and Kirsty still holding on tight.

"Rachel, are you OK?" Kirsty spluttered.

Rachel blinked, but all she could see

was snow. The goblins were squawking and flailing about nearby.

"I'm all right," she said, her voice muffled. "Kirsty, try to reach your spare hand up. We have to show Hana where we are!"

Chapter Six
Hanukkah Fun

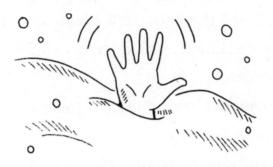

Buried under the snowdrift, it was hard to tell which way was up. Kirsty and Rachel couldn't move their wings, but they stretched their hands up as far as they could. At last . . .

"My fingers have broken through the surface!" said Kirsty.

"Mine too!" said Rachel. "Wave like mad."

They waved as hard as they could, hoping that above the snow, Hana would be searching for them. Seconds later, they felt the fairy's warm hands squeezing theirs. Then the snow fell away, and they sprang up. The hanukkiah was lying beside them.

"Hurray!" Hana cheered, jumping up and down for joy.

The goblins were nearby, shaking snow from their bedraggled clothes. Then the Kirsty goblin spotted the fairies.

"No!" he yelled.

At that moment, Hana reached down and laid her hand on the hanukkiah. It shrank to fairy size, and she hugged it to her chest.

"Now I can put everything right," she said, smiling at Rachel and Kirsty.

"You tricksy, rotten girls," shouted the Rachel goblin.

"Jack Frost is going to yell at us," wailed the Kirsty goblin. "He'll make us wash up for a year."

"Let's hide," the Rachel goblin exclaimed.

They ran off into the darkness, and the fairies exchanged excited smiles. They had done it!

"Jack Frost is going to be crosser with us than ever," said Kirsty.

"Not as cross as Abigail," said Rachel with a sinking feeling. "She still thinks I was rude to her earlier."

"I think I can do something about that, now I've got my magical object back," said Hana with a smile.

She raised her wand, and a wave of sparkling light washed over the house.

"Everyone inside will forget about the goblins' behaviour and the food disappearing," said Hana.

Just then, they heard the back door of the house open.

"Rachel, Kirsty, are you out there?"

called Abigail's voice. "We're about to light the hanukkiah."

"You should go and join in," said Hana. "I have returned the candles that the goblins stole, and now I must get home to Fairyland. Goodbye, girls, and thank you from the bottom of my heart. I couldn't have done it alone."

She blew them each a kiss and then disappeared in a glittering puff of fairy dust. When the sparkles cleared, Rachel and Kirsty were human again. Sharing a smile,

they ran back to the house.

"There you are," said Abigail, pulling them inside. "Come on – this is the best bit."

She led Rachel and Kirsty into the sitting room. The family's hanukkiah was filled with candles again. Everyone smiled at them. It was clear that no one remembered what had happened earlier.

The girls watched as blessings were spoken and all the candles were lit.

"Let us remember the wonderful miracles God did and still does," said Abigail's mum in a happy voice.

There was a moment of thoughtful silence. And then . . .

"Now is it time for the presents?" Miriam asked.

Everyone laughed and Abigail's dad

began to sing. As the music rang out, gifts were handed around. Miriam got a game and Abigail got a book, and all the children were given chocolate coins.

"Hanukkah is a super happy festival," said Rachel, smiling at her best friend. "Thank goodness Jack Frost and his goblins haven't spoiled it. I just hope that we can find the two magical objects that are still missing."

"Don't worry," said Kirsty. "Whatever Jack Frost is planning, we'll be ready to put the magic back into the festivals!"

The End

Now it's time for Kirsty and
Rachel to help...

Brianna the Bee Fairy

Read on for a sneak peek...

"There," said Kirsty Tate, putting the last
badge into her rucksack and zipping it
up. "I've made fifteen Bee Kind badges."

"Me too," said her best friend, Rachel
Walker. "That makes thirty altogether. We
had twenty-two phone calls about the
club, so there should be plenty of badges
for everyone."

The girls shared a happy smile.

"Isn't it exciting that so many people
like our idea?" said Kirsty. "Hopefully
they will all spread the message that the
bees need our help."

Kirsty was staying in Tippington with

Rachel for the first week of the summer holiday. After working on the Tippington peace garden, they had realised how much they enjoyed doing things for the community. When they found out that bees were disappearing from the world, they decided to start a club – Bee Kind – to teach people how to help save the bees. Today was the first meeting. They were starting by placing a water basin in the peace garden, surrounded by bee-friendly flowers.

"Have we got everything we'll need?" asked Rachel.

"Water bottles, badges and the water basin," said Kirsty.

"I've got the sun cream, the seeds and the camera," said Rachel. "Let's go!"

It didn't take them long to walk to the

peace garden. The iron entrance gate had been made specially by the local blacksmith with curving tendrils, leaves and flowers. They pushed it open and walked in.

The peace garden was always a quiet place, but this morning there was no one else there. Brightly coloured flowers nodded in the breeze, and the only sound was the faint tinkle of wind chimes. Marnie, the head gardener, had set aside a flowerbed for the girls to do their planting.

"Oh look, Marnie's left out lots of gardening tools and watering cans for us," said Rachel, slipping her rucksack off her bag. "How kind."

"People should start arriving any minute," said Kirsty, who was keeping an eye on the gate.

"Lots of my friends from school said they'd come along," said Rachel.

They sat cross-legged by the flowerbed and waited . . . and waited . . . and waited.

Read Brianna the Bee Fairy to find out what adventures are in store for Kirsty and Rachel!

RAINBOW
magic

Calling all parents, carers and teachers!
The Rainbow Magic fairies are here to help
your child enter the magical world of reading.
Whatever reading stage they are at, there's
a Rainbow Magic book for everyone!
Here is Lydia the Reading Fairy's guide to
supporting your child's journey at all levels.

Starting Out

1 Our Rainbow Magic Beginner Readers are perfect for first-time readers who are just beginning to develop reading skills and confidence. Approved by teachers, they contain a full range of educational levelling, as well as lively full-colour illustrations.

Developing Readers

2 Rainbow Magic Early Readers contain longer stories and wider vocabulary for building stamina and growing confidence. These are adaptations of our most popular Rainbow Magic stories, specially developed for younger readers in conjunction with an Early Years reading consultant, with full-colour illustrations.

Going Solo

3 The Rainbow Magic chapter books - a mixture of series and one-off specials - contain accessible writing to encourage your child to venture into reading independently. These highly collectible and much-loved magical stories inspire a love of reading to last a lifetime.

www.rainbowmagicbooks.co.uk

"Rainbow Magic got my daughter reading chapter books. Great sparkly covers, cute fairies and traditional stories full of magic that she found impossible to put down" - Mother of Edie (6 years)

"Florence LOVES the Rainbow Magic books. She really enjoys reading now" - Mother of Florence (6 years)

Read along the Reading Rainbow!

Well done – you have completed the book!

This book was worth 1 star.

See how far you have climbed on the Reading Rainbow opposite.
The more books you read, the more stars you can colour in
and the closer you will be to becoming a Royal Fairy!

Do you want to print your own Reading Rainbow?

1) Go to the Rainbow Magic website

2) Download and print out the poster

3) Colour in a star for every book you finish
and climb the Reading Rainbow

4) For every step up the rainbow,
you can download your very own certificate

There's all this and lots more at
rainbowmagicbooks.co.uk

You'll find activities, stories, a special newsletter
AND you can search for the fairy with your name!